P9-DUK-193

ROYAL RESCUES

The Snowy Reindeer

Paula Harrison

illustrated by Olivia Chin Mueller

SCHOLASTIC INC.

For my mum,
who always made Christmas magical

First published in the UK by Nosy Crow
as *Princess of Pets: The Snowy Reindeer* in 2019.

No part of this publication may be reproduced, stored in a retrieval system, or transmitted in any form or by any means, electronic, mechanical, photocopying, recording, or otherwise, without written permission of the publisher. For information regarding permission, write to Feiwel and Friends, an imprint of Macmillan Publishing Group, LLC, 120 Broadway, New York, NY 10271.

ISBN 978-1-338-81172-8

Text copyright © 2019 by Paula Harrison.
Illustrations copyright © 2019 by Olivia Chin Mueller. All rights reserved.
Published by Scholastic Inc., 557 Broadway, New York, NY 10012,
by arrangement with Feiwel and Friends, an imprint of
Macmillan Publishing Group, LLC. SCHOLASTIC and
associated logos are trademarks and/or registered
trademarks of Scholastic Inc.

The publisher does not have any control over and does
not assume any responsibility for author or
third-party websites or their content.

12 11 10 9 8 7 6 5 4 3   22 23 24 25 26

Printed in the U.S.A.   37

First Scholastic printing, November 2021

Book design by Nosy Crow

Chapter One

The Castle
in the Snow

Bea leaned her head out the car
window and a snowflake landed on
her nose. Her tummy fizzed with
excitement. "It's snowing already and
we're not even there yet!"

"Beatrice, what on earth are you
doing?" said her father, King George.
"Close that window at once, before
you catch a cold."

But while Bea closed the car window,

her younger brother,
Alfie, opened another one.
The wind rushed past and a
flurry of snowflakes blew in.

"Hey!" cried Alfie. "I caught
a snowflake on my tongue!"

"Alfie! Dad said don't open the
window." Natasha, their older sister,
leaned over and shut it.

Mr. Humbert, the royal chauffeur,
turned the wheel, and the shiny black
car swept around a corner into a long
driveway. A magnificent castle crowned
with a row of snowy-white turrets came
into view. Fir trees stood on both sides
of the driveway, which sloped upward
to the castle steps.

The king, who was sitting in the
front beside the driver, turned around

to smile at his children. "Here we are! Take your first look at Peruva Castle."

Bea stared up at the snowy castle. It was white and sparkling, as if powdered

sugar had been shaken all over it. She had been excited about this holiday visit to see Great-Aunt Sylvia for weeks and weeks. There would be plenty of time for snowball fights and building snowmen, and that slope down to the field looked perfect for sledding!

Snow never fell at home in Savara because it was so hot and sunny. Here, in the north, they had snow every winter. The snowdrifts were so crisp and deep that you could jump into them and sink until the snow came to the top of your boots!

Bea's mind wandered. She imagined she was swooping down a hill on a sled, holding tight to the reins with her woolly mittens.

Natasha nudged her. "Bea, are you listening? Dad's talking to us."

Bea jumped. "Yes, I'm listening."

"Remember you must *all* be on your very best behavior. Great-Aunt Sylvia is very kind to invite us to stay, and your cousins are little, so you have to set a good example for them," said King George.

Bea smiled. She couldn't wait to see their cousins, Annie and Leo. Annie was three years old, and Leo would be having his first birthday tomorrow. They had wrapped up lots of presents for him. Bea's favorite was the teddy bear with the shiny red ribbon around its neck.

"Natasha, I'm putting you in charge because you're the oldest," the king continued. "I don't want to hear lots of noise and mischief. We're going to be perfect guests for Great-Aunt Sylvia."

"Yes, Dad." Natasha nodded seriously. "I'll make sure nothing goes wrong."

Bea glanced at her sister in alarm. Natasha was already quite bossy about royal rules and manners. She was sure to be even worse now that she was in charge!

The car stopped outside the castle, and Annie came running down the steps, her eyes sparkling. Her parents, Uncle Henry and Aunt Amber, followed with baby Leo. Lastly, Great-Aunt Sylvia came out with her walking stick. She was wearing a rainbow-colored scarf, and she had dyed her hair purple.

Great-Aunt Sylvia was actually Lady Sylvia Nibbs, whose family had owned Peruva Castle for hundreds of years. Bea liked her a lot because she wore brightly colored outfits, played rock and roll very loudly, and didn't seem to care what anyone thought. Bea remembered dancing along to the music when she was younger.

Bea climbed out of the car, and little Annie leapt at her. "Hi, Bea! Do you like my new bobble hat?" The little girl pointed to her blue hat with its fluffy pom-pom.

"It looks great!" Bea hugged her back.

"Thanks for inviting us to stay, Aunt Sylvia." King George kissed Lady Sylvia's cheek before saying hello to Uncle Henry and Aunt Amber.

"It's wonderful to see you!" said

Great-Aunt Sylvia, smiling. "Children, come here and let me look at you all. Goodness, Princess Beatrice! It's amazing how much you've grown!"

"Can we play in the snow?" Alfie jumped around, trying to catch more snowflakes on his tongue.

"Alfie!" Natasha made a grab for him. "We've only just got here."

"There'll be plenty of time for playing in the snow later," said their great-aunt. "Come inside and warm up first. I've asked Mr. Upply to fetch us hot chocolate and cinnamon buns."

A gloomy-faced man in a black suit appeared at the front door. "The refreshments are ready in the parlor, Your Ladyship."

"Thank you, Upply." Lady Sylvia turned around slowly, leaning on her stick.

As Bea followed her into the house, she looked around eagerly for animals. "Great-Aunt Sylvia, do you keep any pets?" she asked hopefully.

"No, my dear," replied Lady Sylvia. "But there is a little robin that likes to come and perch on the parlor windowsill. I sprinkle crumbs there for him. I'll point him out to you sometime."

"Oh!" Bea's heart sank. She had really hoped Great-Aunt Sylvia might have a dog or a cat she could play with.

Even though Bea was animal-mad, she wasn't allowed to have any pets in her room at Ruby Palace. Her father had always been quite strict about this rule, saying, *Beatrice, a palace is no place for a pet.* Bea had felt quite sad about it at first, but then she'd begun looking after any animals that needed her help. She'd rescued Tiger, a gorgeous kitten, and Rosie, a playful puppy. She couldn't imagine spending the whole holiday without any animals around.

Bea tried to smile as she followed her great-aunt into the parlor. Soon everyone was sitting beside the crackling fire, drinking mugs of hot chocolate and eating warm cinnamon buns. Baby Leo began to gurgle, and everyone chatted happily. Even Natasha stopped looking serious and smiled as she braided Annie's ponytail.

"It's so nice to have you all here together!" Great-Aunt Sylvia beamed, handing Bea the empty bun plate. "Would you go to the kitchen and fetch some more buns, please, Princess

Beatrice? Obviously, some of us are *very* hungry." She glanced at Alfie, who was cramming a third bun into his mouth.

Bea nodded and took the plate. She hurried through the drawing room and the library, following the long chain of rooms that led to the kitchen. Fires were lit in all the hearths, and there were boxes of shiny streamers ready to hang up around the walls. The sunshine made the snow on the windowsills sparkle.

Bea sighed. Then she gave herself a shake. She had been so excited to come to the snowy castle—and she was still really glad to be here—but she missed Rosie and Tiger. If only there was an animal here she could make friends with!

Chapter Two
A Flash of Orange Fur

Once everyone had warmed up and finished all the buns and hot chocolate, Great-Aunt Sylvia told the children they could go out in the snow. Bea rushed to get her coat and boots. Then she pulled on a thick bobble hat and tied a red woolly scarf around her neck.

"I can't wait to build a snowman!" cried Annie, putting her boots on the wrong feet.

"Those aren't right, Annie." Natasha pointed to the boots before yelling out the door, "Alfie, come back! You don't even have a coat on!"

"Here, I'll help you." Bea crouched down to swap Annie's boots onto the right feet. "Don't forget your gloves. It's really frosty out there!" She smiled at the little girl before pulling on her own gloves and stepping outside.

The castle garden lay under a thick, white snow blanket. Delicate lines of frost clung to every leaf and branch, sparkling in the sunlight. Here and there, little bird prints were scattered across the whiteness.

Bea took a few giant steps across the garden, listening to the snow crunch under her Wellington boots. Then a snowball from Alfie whizzed past her ear.

Bea laughed and scooped up a lump of snow. Squashing it between her gloves, she threw it at her brother. Soon Natasha and Annie joined in, and there were snowballs flying everywhere.

Bea and the others played in the snowy garden for hours. There was a game of tag, leaving footprints all over the place. They also made a snowman with a twig mouth, two little stones for eyes, and a carrot nose that Natasha fetched from the kitchen. Last of all, they made a snow dog, sitting beside the snowman, with long ears and a big white tail.

The sun disappeared behind a huge gray cloud.

"My hands are cold!" said Annie suddenly.

"Mine too! Let's go inside," said Natasha. "Come on—you'll feel warmer once you've had another hot chocolate."

"But we didn't get the sleds out!" cried Alfie, tugging at the door to the shed. "I want to go sledding."

"We can do that tomorrow," said Natasha. "We're here for three days." But Alfie kept pulling on the latch. The shed door flew open with a creaky groan and a pile of flowerpots fell out. "Alfie, now look what you've done!"

Alfie made a face and kicked a mound of snow.

Bea caught a flicker of movement at the corner of the shed. Then there was a flash of orange fur just behind a pile of logs stacked against the shed wall. Was that a dog . . . or maybe a fox? She watched the logs carefully, but the creature didn't move again. She hoped they hadn't scared it with all the shouting.

"I'll tidy up and close the shed," she told Natasha quickly. "You take the others inside. I'll be there in a minute."

"Don't be too long, Bea." Natasha held Annie's hand as she set off across the garden. Alfie stomped behind them, scowling.

Bea picked up the flowerpots and stacked them neatly. Once the others were gone, she moved toward the log pile. The wood had been stored under the overhanging roof to keep it free from snow. As Bea got nearer, there was a scrabbling of claws, and a very large orange cat with a thick tail leapt out from behind the logs. The animal hissed, barring her way, and its spiky whiskers stiffened.

Bea stepped back in surprise. At first glance the animal had seemed fox-sized, so she hadn't expected a cat at all. "Hello! You're enormous, aren't you? Where are you from? Do you live nearby?" She held out her hand, expecting the cat to want to be stroked.

The orange cat gave a low snarl and flexed its claws.

"Don't worry—
I won't hurt you," Bea
said soothingly.
"I love cats.
I know
a kitten
called

Tiger, and we're great friends! What's
your name? Maybe I could call you
Ginger."

Ginger's snarl rose into a yowl, and
its tail flicked fiercely. It stared at Bea,
its dark yellow eyes narrowing into
thin slits.

Bea drew her hand back quickly.
This cat wasn't very friendly at all. She
wasn't sure where it came from—
Great-Aunt Sylvia had said there were
no animals at the castle—but it didn't
look like it needed rescuing. Bea didn't
think she dared pick it up, anyway.

She was about to leave when Ginger
jumped on top of the woodpile and stared
down the gap between the logs. The cat
gave a low mew and scraped at the wood,
as if it was trying to reach something.
Bea peered into the hole, and her heart

jumped as a pair of scared brown eyes stared back.

"Ginger, what have you found?" Bea looked closer, ignoring the cat's hissing.

A pale brown furry face looked up at her. The creature had soft velvety ears

and a patch of darker fur on its nose. Between its ears, two small antlers poked up.

"A reindeer!" Bea stared in astonishment. "How did you get in there?"

The reindeer pricked up its ears and twitched its fluffy white tail. Ginger grew excited and scratched the logs with its sharp claws. The reindeer shrank back, its nose trembling.

"Stop it!" Bea reached for the cat, wondering if the naughty animal had chased the reindeer under the logs in the first place.

Ginger slipped past her fingers and started squeezing under the pile of wood. Bea was suddenly afraid of what the cat might do. Ginger was so fierce and the reindeer was so frightened.

She clapped her hands at the cat. "Shoo! Go and find something else to chase."

Ginger sidled away with a low yowl. The cat sat down in the snow a short distance away and began licking its paws, stopping every few seconds to throw Bea an annoyed look.

"Hi, little reindeer!" Bea crouched down and peered between the logs. "What are you doing down there?"

The reindeer wriggled, and its dark brown nose twitched anxiously. Bea noticed that one of its hooves was stuck between two logs. The animal's eyes flashed with panic as it tried to pull itself free.

"You poor thing! Hold still and I'll help you." Bea leaned over the log pile, trying to figure out what to do. The logs looked heavy, and she didn't want the whole pile to tumble down and hurt the reindeer.

She took hold of each log, rolling it carefully aside. Then she reached down into the space and gently pulled the reindeer's hoof free. The animal shrank back a little. Then it sniffed at her sleeve.

"There you are—free at last!" Bea lifted the reindeer out of the woodpile and set him down on the snow. His fur was soft and pale, and he wobbled a little on his thin legs. Bea stroked his head gently and stared around the snowy garden. He must be a wild reindeer, but where was the rest of his herd?

"Shouldn't you be with your mother?" she said, and the reindeer twitched his soft ears.

Bea was just wondering whether to

fetch the snowman's carrot nose for him to eat, when she spotted Ginger skulking near the shed door. She quickly gathered the baby reindeer into her arms. He wriggled for a moment before snuggling against her coat.

She frowned worriedly. The sun was

setting, and the shadows of the trees stretched across the snow like spiky hands. What was she supposed to do? If she left the reindeer here, Ginger was sure to chase him again. The big cat had sharp claws and a mean look in its eyes.

Bea hugged the little animal tighter. She *had* to take him inside! It was the only way she would know he was safe. She wrapped her coat around him and hid his head underneath her scarf. Then she hurried back to the castle door. Ginger stared after her grumpily before padding away across the snow.

Chapter Three
Keeping a Secret

Bea crept into the castle with the reindeer tucked snugly into the top of her coat. There were voices in the parlor, and the smell of hot chocolate drifted into the hall.

Bea pulled off her Wellington boots and tiptoed to the stairs. "What shall I call you?" she whispered. "Maybe Woody, because you were hiding in the woodpile."

"There you are, Beatrice!" Great-Aunt Sylvia came past with an armful of sparkly streamers. "We're just about to put up the decorations for Leo's party tomorrow. Would you like to come and help us?"

The baby reindeer wriggled under Bea's coat, and two velvety ears popped out from the top of her scarf. Bea looked at her great-aunt in alarm. Luckily, Lady Sylvia was busy pinning up a streamer.

"Yes, please!" gabbled Bea, dashing up the stairs. "I'll be back in a minute!"

"Your guest bedroom is just on the left, dear," her great-aunt called after her.

Bea hurried to the room where she and Natasha would be sleeping. Throwing off her coat and scarf, she set the reindeer down on the bed's pink quilt.

The guest room was clean and

bright, with a crystal vase full of flowers
on the night table.

"Well, you can't sleep in here. Natasha
would never approve!" Bea told the
reindeer as she unzipped her suitcase,
looking for something to use as a towel.

The reindeer settled down on the
bed, his nose twitching. Bea knelt
beside him and stroked his soft coat.

She had to find out where his herd had gone. In the meantime, she needed somewhere safe to keep him.

Slipping out the door, she went along the passage, peeping into each room. At last she found a small room at the end of the corridor with no bed inside. Boxes were stacked against the wall, and there was an old sofa with faded cushions. Bea's heart rose. It looked as if Great-Aunt Sylvia was just using the room to store things. That made it an excellent place to hide a reindeer.

"What are you doing?" asked Alfie.

Bea jumped. "Alfie, don't sneak up on me like that!" She saw that Alfie was holding a large cardboard box, and an idea popped into her head. "Hand me the box. I'll store it in here for you."

Alfie held on to it. "Leo's birthday

presents are in here, and I'm supposed to put it somewhere safe."

"I'll look after them." Bea took hold of the box, but Alfie wouldn't let go.

"I want to do it! Anyway, Dad says you have to come downstairs."

"I need the box for something," Bea told him. Alfie made a stubborn face, so she added, "It's something important! I'll show you—but you have to promise not to tell."

"I won't!" said Alfie eagerly.

Bea led Alfie back down the hallway and opened the door to the guest room. The reindeer was standing on the edge of the bed, happily chewing the flowers on the night table and leaving behind a bunch of bare stalks.

"A reindeer!" Alfie dumped the cardboard box on the floor and ran over to the animal. "Where did you get him from?"

Bea explained about the log pile and the orange cat. "So I just need somewhere to keep him, and the box would make a good reindeer bed." She lifted the reindeer into her arms, and Alfie stroked his fur.

"Okay, you can have the box, on one condition." Alfie folded his arms. "I want to choose the reindeer's name."

"All right . . . but please don't call him Firestorm," said Bea, remembering what her brother had wanted to call the puppy she'd found in the palace garden that spring. "I think Woody would be nice!"

"Boring!" Alfie took hold of the

reindeer and hugged him tight. "I want to call him Marshmallow. Look at his stubby little tail—it's exactly the size of a marshmallow!"

Bea smiled. "Actually, that's a pretty good name. Hello, Marshmallow! I'm going to find lots of vegetables for you so you can grow big and strong." She tickled him under the chin.

"He's already growing big and strong on those flowers," Alfie pointed out.

Bea opened the cardboard box and put baby Leo's birthday presents carefully on the table. Then she took the towel from her suitcase and laid it in the box to make a nice soft bed for the reindeer.

Alfie found a pen in Natasha's suitcase and wrote *Marshmallow's House* on the side of the box. Then

Bea placed the reindeer gently inside. Marshmallow stood there, wobbling on his thin legs and looking surprised, until Bea gave him the rest of the flowers to nibble.

"Can you watch him for me?" she asked Alfie. "I'm going to fetch him some food."

"Sure!" Alfie crouched beside the box, drawing pictures of leaping reindeer across the sides.

Bea hurried down the stairs and went straight to the kitchen. Mr. Upply was there, filling the kettle with water.

"Can I help you, Princess Beatrice?" The butler lifted a bushy eyebrow.

Bea was a bit shy around Mr. Upply. He seemed so glum all the time, and he moved about the kitchen slower than a tortoise. "Um . . . I was just looking for a healthy snack." She blushed. She couldn't tell him the snack was actually for Marshmallow. "I don't think Great-Aunt Sylvia will mind me helping myself."

The butler got some teacups from the cupboard, almost in slow motion. "Very well, then. There is some fruit in the bowl over there, and if you like breadsticks, you might find some of those in the pantry."

Bea edged toward a basket filled with vegetables and stuffed her pockets with cabbage, spinach, and broccoli.

She hid the vegetables quickly before the butler turned around. "Thank you, I've got plenty now." She darted down the hallway, her pockets bulging, and ran straight into Alfie, who had an armful of streamers. "Alfie! You should be upstairs watching the you-know-what!"

"Natasha called me. I had to come or she would have gotten suspicious." Alfie scowled. "And I'm sick of everyone bossing me around!" He marched off, dragging the streamers along the floor behind him.

Bea raced up the stairs, taking them two at a time. Her heart sank when she saw that the door to the guest room was open. Taking a deep breath, she stepped inside.

Marshmallow's velvety ears were

poking over the top of the box, and Annie was crouching beside him. "I found a reindeer," she told Bea proudly. "I think he must be magic!"

Bea couldn't help smiling at her cousin. "He's very cute, isn't he? He's called Marshmallow."

The reindeer sniffed Annie's fingers and gave a little bleat, making her giggle.

Bea rubbed her forehead. What was she going to do now that Annie knew about Marshmallow? Keeping this reindeer a secret was turning out to be trickier than she'd thought!

Chapter Four
Annie and
the Reindeer

Bea crouched down beside Annie.
"Would you like to feed Marshmallow?
I've brought him some vegetables to eat."

Annie's face lit up. "Yes, please!"

Bea emptied her pockets of the
broccoli, spinach, and cabbage. She lifted
the baby reindeer out of the box and
held him close while Annie fed him one
leaf at a time. Marshmallow finished all
the cabbage and most of the spinach.

Just as he reached forward to try some broccoli, Annie grabbed him for a cuddle. The reindeer began to struggle, his little hooves kicking in the air.

"I think he wants to fly," breathed Annie, her eyes lighting up. "Go on—fly, Marshmallow!"

"I really don't think he can fly," said Bea, trying to take the reindeer back.

Annie held on tighter. "He might! I've seen pictures of flying reindeer in books."

"That was probably just a story. I think you should let him go . . ."

Annie pouted. "Maybe we just need to know the magic word to help him."

Tired of being squeezed, the reindeer broke free of Annie's arms and skittered out the door, his white tail bobbing. Bea jumped up in alarm and gave

chase, managing to catch the little
animal halfway down the corridor. She
took some spinach from her pocket
and stroked Marshmallow's coat gently
as he ate the leaves.

Once she'd calmed him down, she
brought the box she'd prepared to the
storeroom and settled Marshmallow
inside. She fetched a small bowl of

water from the bathroom and left it for the reindeer along with the rest of the spinach and broccoli.

"Let me hold him again!" cried Annie, as Marshmallow lay down inside the box.

"Shhh! Look—he's going to sleep now," Bea told her. "It would be mean to wake him up." She steered her little cousin outside and pulled the door to the storeroom shut.

Annie's face darkened. "Why can't I pet him? Why won't you let me see him, Bea?"

"You can see him again later," Bea promised. "But I don't think we should tell the grown-ups about him just yet. They're busy thinking about Leo's birthday party tomorrow. As soon as I've found Marshmallow's family,

I can explain everything. Shall we go and see if they've put up the birthday decorations yet?"

Annie nodded. "I wish it was my party! Leo's only a baby, and he doesn't even know it's his birthday." She skipped off downstairs, singing to herself.

Bea followed her more slowly. She knew she couldn't keep Marshmallow in the castle for long. The little reindeer needed to be with his herd, but how was she going to find out where they'd gone?

She thought hard about it as she went downstairs. The parlor and the hallway twinkled with silver streamers and a huge HAPPY BIRTHDAY banner hung over the fireplace.

Natasha came out of the library clutching a pile of red napkins and stopped when she saw Bea. "Where have you *been*? There was lots of tidying up to do before the party tomorrow. We needed your help!"

Bea hesitated. If she was going to tell everyone about Marshmallow, maybe she should start with her sister . . . except Natasha looked so upset. "I can help now, if you want?"

"It's too late now!" huffed Natasha, putting the napkins down. "Why did you take so long? I bet you went on that sled on your own!"

"I didn't—I promise!" said Bea. "But while I was by the shed, I found something amazing—"

"Natasha!" Great-Aunt Sylvia called from the parlor.

Natasha rushed off, saying over her shoulder, "Tell me later, okay? And can you fold those napkins?"

Bea folded the pile of red napkins. Then she went to the window and stared at the gleaming white garden. Snow lined every leaf and branch on the trees, and icicles as clear as glass hung from the shed roof. On one side, the garden was bordered by a small forest. On the other, there was a hill that looked perfect for sledding.

Bea felt a thrill of excitement. There must be a really great view from that hill. Maybe, if she climbed to the top, she'd be able to spot the reindeer herd! Without stopping to think, she dashed into the hallway and pulled on her coat and boots before rushing out of the castle.

Bea's footsteps were muffled by the

snow, and the cold pinched her fingers. She pulled her gloves on quickly as she headed through the garden gate and up the hill.

The snow lay even more thickly on the steep slope, and Bea stepped into snowdrifts several times, sinking into them to the top of her boots. Snow seeped down into her socks, turning her feet to icicles, but she trudged on, trying to ignore the cold.

She had almost reached the top when the snow started to fall again. At first, Bea admired the dancing flakes, catching them on her glove. Then, as the snow thickened, she realized that the woods and fields all around were disappearing from view. A rabbit popped

its head out of a snowy burrow before vanishing underground again.

Bea sighed and turned around. There was no way she would spot the reindeer herd in this weather. She would just have to wait until the snow stopped. She stumbled back across the garden through the whirling snow. As she opened the door and stamped the snow off her boots, the delicious smell of dinner drifted through the castle.

Bea hung up her coat, put on her slippers, and rushed to the stairs. If she was quick, maybe she could spend some time with Marshmallow before she was called down for dinner. "Hello, Marshmallow! Are you all right?" She peeked into the room where she'd left the baby reindeer, and her stomach gave a terrible lurch.

The box had a hole in the side and

bits of chewed-up cardboard were scattered across the carpet.

"Marshmallow! What happened?" Bea dashed over to the box, discovering it was empty.

She searched around the room, peering under chairs and behind a chest of drawers. Where had the reindeer gone? He had seemed so happy and sleepy

when she'd left him, but he must have woken up and escaped into the rest of the castle. Maybe he was searching for more vegetables to eat.

Bea bit her lip. The grown-ups would be so angry if they found him before she got the chance to explain everything. She had to find the little animal quickly, before they both got into a lot of trouble!

Chapter Five
Marshmallow Gets into Mischief

Bea rushed from one room to the next like a whirlwind. She peeped under beds, inside suitcases, and behind wardrobes. Marshmallow was so small he could easily squeeze into a tiny space somewhere. "Marshmallow, please come out," she called. "I promise I'll find you some lovely, juicy broccoli!"

She followed a trail of tiny bits of cardboard down the corridor. Her tummy did a somersault when she heard rustling in the guest room. "Marshmallow!" she cried, bounding through the doorway.

"Bea?" Natasha turned around with a frown darker than a rain cloud. "I thought you and Alfie were looking after Leo's presents. Just look at them!"

Bea stared in dismay. The silver-and-blue wrapping paper around the presents was chewed all over. The teddy bear's face was poking out of its box, and the end of the shiny red ribbon it wore was

tattered and torn. Bea knew at once that Marshmallow had nibbled them all.

"I can explain everything!" she said.

Natasha folded her arms. "Does this have something to do with an animal?"

Bea stared at her sister in surprise. "How did you know?"

"Because it *always* has something to do with an animal." Natasha sighed. "What is it this time? A chipmunk? A guinea pig? You know what Dad will say. Bringing an animal into our palace at home is bad enough, but when you're a guest in someone else's house, it's really rude!"

Bea went red. She knew Natasha was right. She shouldn't have brought Marshmallow into her great-aunt's home, but the poor reindeer had looked so cold and alone.

Natasha put down the birthday presents. "You'd better tell me, Bea! Are you hiding the animal somewhere? I can help you take it outside again."

"It's a little reindeer called Marshmallow," Bea told her. "I made a cozy bed for him using the box that the presents came in, but he's run away somewhere."

"A reindeer!" cried Natasha. "But where did he come from?"

"I found him in the woodpile next to the shed," explained Bea. "I guess there must be a reindeer herd close by, but I haven't found them yet. It's freezing outside, and there was a mean-looking orange cat—"

"Natasha! Beatrice! Time for dinner," Aunt Amber called from downstairs.

"We'll talk about this later," hissed

Natasha as they hurried to the dining room. "But you'd better figure out where the animal's gone, and if anything else is chewed, I'm telling Dad right away."

Bea gave her sister an annoyed look. It was typical of Natasha to be more worried about a bit of mess than about keeping the poor reindeer safe.

The dining room sparkled with shiny streamers, and the fire crackling in the hearth cast a golden glow across the floor. Bea sat down beside Alfie, who was helping himself to extra roast potatoes. Mr. Upply brought in a jug of gravy and dishes of carrots and peas.

"I want Marshmallow!" said Annie loudly.

"Shh, honey!" said Aunt Amber. "You can't have any sweets until you've finished your dinner."

Bea turned red. She knew Annie was talking about the reindeer. Alfie burst into giggles, and Natasha gave him a very stern look.

"The decorations for Leo's party look great," Uncle Henry said as he passed the carrots to Bea. "Thanks for helping out, everyone."

Bea took the carrots. She was just about to pass them to Alfie when a soft tapping noise came from the hallway. Was that the sound of reindeer hooves? Bea longed to run out and check, but she couldn't think of a reason to leave the table. She ate her roast potatoes quickly, hoping she could finish and be excused.

The grown-ups kept talking about plans for Leo's birthday party. Mr. Upply had just brought in a second jug of gravy when a jumpy string of notes came from the piano in the parlor.

King George looked up in surprise. "Who's playing the piano, Aunt Sylvia? Does your cook like to play?"

"I don't think so." Lady Sylvia turned to the butler. "Upply, is that Mrs. Miller on the piano?"

"No, Your Ladyship. She's busy preparing the chocolate brownies," replied Mr. Upply.

"How very strange!" said Lady Sylvia. "We're all here together, and there's no one else in the castle."

"Maybe it's a ghost!" said Alfie, grinning.

The piano music sounded as if someone was walking their fingers up and down the keys. Then it grew faster and jerkier, leaping from note to note.

Bea stopped with a forkful of carrots
halfway to her mouth. The music
made her think an animal might be
scampering up and down the piano
keys!

"I know what it is!" said Lady Sylvia,
beaming. "It must be Jasper. He does
sneak into the castle from time to time."

"Who's Jasper?" asked Natasha.

"He's the big orange cat that lives
in the house at the bottom of the hill,"
replied Lady Sylvia. "He can be a bit
of a grumpy old thing, bless him, but
he loves to pad around the castle and
lounge in front of the fire. I'm not even
sure how he manages to get inside!"

Bea's stomach turned cold. The
orange cat was inside the castle! What
if he found Marshmallow and scared
the poor reindeer? She jumped to her

feet. "Great-Aunt, can I be excused for a moment?"

"Of course, my dear." Lady Sylvia smiled. "Your father's been telling me how much you like animals. I'm sure you want to go and pet Jasper."

"I'll come, too!" Natasha rose to her feet, shooting a look at her sister. "I ... Er ... I love animals, too. Don't I, Bea?"

Bea didn't stop to reply. Her feet thudded as she raced out into the hall.

Chapter Six
The Tracks in the Snow

Bea flung herself through the parlor door. A lumpy orange cat looked up from where he was sitting on top of the piano. It was the same cat that Bea had seen in the garden, trying to pounce on the reindeer. This must be Jasper. He gave Bea a cold stare and then went back to washing his paws.

Natasha caught up with her. "You've got to calm down, Bea! You're going to make everyone suspicious, and then they'll find out about the reindeer."

"I thought you wanted the grown-ups to know about Marshmallow," said Bea in surprise.

Natasha looked awkward. "Well . . . if Dad finds out, he'll be upset with both of us. Remember how he said I was in charge because I'm the oldest."

"Oh!" Bea felt a twinge of sympathy for her sister. "I'm really sorry! I didn't mean to get you into trouble."

Jasper crashed onto the piano keys with an earsplitting *bong* before jumping to the floor. He prowled across the rug, narrowing his eyes as he passed Bea and Natasha. Then he raised his nose and sniffed the air. Bea grabbed him as he crept toward the door.

"What are you doing?" cried Natasha. "I thought you liked cats."

"I do! But this orange one was chasing Marshmallow. He's the reason I had to bring the reindeer inside." Bea fought to hold on to the wriggling cat. "If we let him stay here, he might do it again."

Jasper gave a low yowl ending with a hiss. He struggled harder, and his sharp claws raked through the air. Twisting around, he scraped a claw across Bea's arm, and she let him go in surprise. She pushed up her sleeve and rubbed the scratch mark on her skin. The orange cat slunk under the coffee table and glared at the girls with fierce yellow eyes.

"You should leave him alone!" said Natasha. "His sense of smell is sure to be better than ours—he could lead us straight to the reindeer."

"I hadn't thought of that!" Bea
stood back. "Go on then, Jasper. Find
Marshmallow for us."

Jasper watched them suspiciously
for a few minutes. Then he crept out of
his hiding place and headed down the
hall. Bea and Natasha followed him

at a safe distance. The cat nosed around the library, sniffing in all the corners, before prowling around the hall closet.

Bea opened the closet door, hoping that Marshmallow was inside, but there was just a mop and bucket and a creaky-looking ironing board. The mop crashed to the floor, and Jasper sprang away with a hiss.

"Where did he go?" asked Natasha.

Bea stared around the hall. "He must have run into the kitchen."

The girls raced after the cat, nearly bumping into a rosy-cheeked woman picking up a tray of chocolate brownies.

"Careful, girls!" said the cook, laughing. "I see you're excited to have dessert!"

"Oops, sorry!" gasped Bea. "Did you see an orange cat come this way?"

"Is Jasper on the prowl again?"
The cook smiled. "I haven't seen him,
but don't worry! He usually turns up
again, especially when he wants some
treats. I'm Mrs. Miller, by the way."

"Pleased to meet you! I'm Natasha
and this is Bea." Natasha picked up a
second tray of brownies. "Would you
like us to help you with these?"

"That's very kind!" Mrs. Miller
pointed to a tub of ice cream. "Could
one of you bring the strawberry ice
cream? And there's an ice cream scoop
in the drawer."

Bea hung back for a moment as
Mrs. Miller and Natasha left with the
trays of brownies. She took the ice
cream scoop out of the drawer before
searching around the kitchen. Jasper
had to be somewhere nearby!

At last, she found the plump orange cat crouched beside the fridge. Jasper swished his tail angrily as she knelt down to see what he was staring at. She couldn't see Marshmallow anywhere, but Jasper pricked up his ears as if he was listening to something.

"Bea, we need the ice cream!" called Natasha.

"Don't move, Jasper!" Bea rushed down the hall and gave the ice cream and the scoop to her sister, before racing back to the kitchen.

The orange cat had vanished. Bea

searched the kitchen, but there was no
sign of him. Her shoulders slumped.
She'd hoped she might be close to
finding Marshmallow, but now she
would have to start all over again.
The castle was huge, and Jasper and
Marshmallow could be anywhere!

A breath of cold air sent a shiver
down her neck. She followed the
passage leading away from the kitchen
and found the back door slightly ajar.
The wind whistled outside, and the
door creaked as it moved in the breeze.

Bea pulled the door wider, and a
cluster of snowflakes blew into her face.
She rubbed her cold arms. Had Jasper
gone outside? But why would he want
to leave the warm castle? Most cats
would rather stay inside by the fire.

She was about to close the door when

she spotted a trail of paw prints leading off into the snow. Were they Jasper's tracks? She peered into the darkness.

There was a line of hoofprints alongside the paw tracks. They were fainter and more spread out, as if the animal had been scampering away in a hurry.

Bea marched outside, ignoring the freezing snow seeping into her slippers. The first set of prints definitely belonged to a cat—each one had four toes around a larger pad—and the hoofprints could easily belong to a reindeer.

Bea took a gulp of icy air. The hoof tracks must be Marshmallow's! No wonder Jasper had decided to leave the warm castle behind. He'd finally found the little reindeer and had started chasing him. Marshmallow was all alone and in danger, lost in the snow.

Chapter Seven
A Moonlit Chase

Bea followed the animal tracks across the snow, her heart thumping. Poor Marshmallow must be so cold and scared out here in the dark. Jasper could have chased him a long way from the castle, and meanwhile snowflakes were whirling out of the velvet-black sky. Bea knew she had to find the little reindeer before the falling snow covered his tracks altogether.

She struggled through the snowdrifts, desperately scanning the snow for tracks. Her furry slippers became soaking wet, and her feet felt like blocks of ice. Running back inside, she went to the hallway to fetch her coat and Wellington boots.

"Where are you going?" Natasha appeared just as Bea was pulling on her boots. "Great-Aunt Sylvia is asking if you're all right."

"I found animal tracks by the back door," Bea said breathlessly. "Marshmallow's out there in the dark, and Jasper's gone, too. I'm going after them!"

"Wait—I'll come with you!" Natasha darted back into the dining room, and then returned to grab her coat. "I told them we wouldn't be long. Bea, you can't go out there without a hat, scarf, and gloves. You'll freeze!"

Bea rummaged around for her hat and gloves. There was no point arguing with her sister. It would just waste more time. She stuck the hat on lopsidedly. "I'm ready!"

"Me too!" Natasha took a flashlight from the hall closet, and together the girls ran out into the night.

The snow had stopped falling, and a deep midwinter hush had settled on the castle garden. A full moon slid from behind a cloud, turning the snow into a carpet of sparkling silver. Suddenly, the castle seemed like a frost palace, and the stars in the night sky glittered like tiny crystals of ice.

Bea stared at the footprints from earlier, leading across the lawn to the

snowman. The cat and reindeer tracks
led the opposite way, toward the trees.

"I just know that cat is chasing Marshmallow again. Look how his paw prints follow the reindeer's!"

"You can't blame Jasper." Natasha swept the flashlight beam along the line of paw prints. "Cats like to chase things—it's in their nature."

They followed the zigzagging animal tracks past the shed and across the garden into a cluster of pine trees. Something rustled close by. Bea grabbed the flashlight and shone it into the trees. An owl with dappled brown feathers stared back from a nearby branch, its orange eyes glowing in the dark.

"It's only an owl," she sighed.

Natasha took the flashlight back. "Let's keep going and see where the tracks lead."

They trekked deeper into the woods. The animal tracks circled around the trees, twisting and turning through the prickly undergrowth. Cat prints mixed with the hoof marks until there was a mass of jumbled tracks. A horrible feeling fluttered in Bea's chest. "It looks like they had a fight. Do you think Jasper pounced on poor Marshmallow and scratched him?"

"No, we would have heard something," said Natasha. "I think the reindeer is hiding—we just have to find him before the cat does."

The woods became thicker, and the closely growing trees blocked the moonlight, making the tracks harder to see. At last, Bea found a clear set of hoofprints. Then a whisper of wind made the pine trees sway, and a heap of snow slid off the nearest branch, covering the tracks completely.

"I've lost Marshmallow's hoofprints!" Bea ran around and around, peering into the snowdrifts. "I can't see where they went."

"Stop it, Bea!" called Natasha. "You're going to step on the tracks."

Bea didn't stop. She was picturing Marshmallow—cold and hungry, and trying to hide from the cat. Her foot caught on a tree stump hidden by the snow. She lost her balance, grabbing Natasha's arm as she fell, and they both toppled over. The flashlight flew out of Natasha's hand and struck a branch, bringing a pile of snow down on top of them.

"Urgh!" cried Natasha. "Now I've got snow down my neck."

"I'm sorry!" Bea wiped icy water away from her mouth.

"This is such a complete disaster!" stormed Natasha, struggling to her feet. "How did I let you drag me out here? I should have known it was useless!"

"It's not useless. Marshmallow needs our help." Bea stared at her sister in dismay. Natasha was awful when she got into one of her moods. "I can look for him by myself if you want."

"If you're out here by yourself, you'll only get into more trouble." Natasha fished the flashlight out of the snow and marched off through the trees.

They searched the woods for a long time, but they couldn't find the tracks again. The owl hooted nearby, and the wind grew stronger, whipping flurries of snowflakes off the branches.

"I think we should go back inside, Bea," Natasha said at last. "It's getting late, and Dad will wonder what we're doing. I expect Jasper got tired of chasing the reindeer and went back to the palace kitchen."

Bea's heart sank as she followed her sister back to the castle. She wished she'd kept a closer eye on Marshmallow. Then he would still be safe and warm inside the castle. She knew the little reindeer still needed her. He was much too small to be out here alone in the snow.

The kitchen door had been closed and locked, so they made their way to the front steps. Bea turned back for one last look at the snowy nighttime garden. She felt as if a huge stone had sunk to the bottom of her stomach.

"Come on!" Natasha held the door open for Bea.

"Look, there's Jasper!" Bea pointed

to the lumpy orange cat sitting in the middle of the snowy lawn. Jasper's tail was waving wildly as he stared at the snowman they'd made earlier that day.

Bea caught her breath. If Jasper was here, did that mean Marshmallow was close by, too? She ran down the steps so quickly that she skidded on the ice at the bottom. She landed heavily in the snow, and her red bobble hat flew off. Scrambling to her feet, she kept on running.

Jasper gave a hiss when he saw her and arched his back. Then he switched his glare back to the snowman and the smaller snow dog beside it.

"What's the matter, Jasper? It's just a snowman." Bea glanced at the snowy figure and shivered. The snowman's stone eyes seemed to glint in the moonlight, as if he was alive. She gave herself a shake. It was just the darkness making everything seem strange and spooky.

Jasper prowled over to the snow dog and gave another hiss. Suddenly, a furry nose poked over the snow dog's shoulder and two velvety ears pricked up. Hiding behind the snow dog was the little pale brown reindeer.

"Marshmallow! I've missed you."
Bea ran to hug the little reindeer,
stumbling in the thick snow.

Jasper leapt right onto the snow
dog's back and clambered toward
Marshmallow. The little reindeer froze,
his eyes wide with fright.

"Naughty kitty!" Natasha ran up,
panting, and grabbed Jasper firmly
with a hand under his tummy. "You
shouldn't scare Marshmallow like that."

Bea scooped up Marshmallow. "Don't
worry, you're safe now!" she murmured
into his soft brown fur. "I promise I'll
take good care of you and get you as
many pieces of broccoli as you want!"

Chapter Eight
A Reindeer Hotel

When Bea opened the castle door with
Marshmallow snuggled in her arms, she
found the hallway bustling with people.
King George was hopping around,
trying to pull on his Wellingtons. Alfie
and Annie were begging to be allowed
outside. Baby Leo was cooing in Uncle
Henry's arms. Mr. Upply stood behind
them all, shaking his head and muttering
about rowdy children.

"Where ARE those girls? I thought they'd just gone upstairs to their room." King George gave his Wellingtons a huge tug and hopped so hard that he stumbled into the hall closet, knocking over the mop and bucket.

"It's all right—here they are!" cried Great-Aunt Sylvia. "My goodness, Beatrice! You're completely covered in snow . . . and what is that animal you're holding?"

"Marshmallow!" shrieked Annie, flinging herself at Bea.

"This is Marshmallow, and we found Jasper, too." Bea pointed to the orange cat struggling in Natasha's arms.

"What a pretty reindeer!" Lady Sylvia beamed. "He must belong to the herd I saw on the edge of the woods a few days ago. Where did you find him?"

"He was stuck under the log pile by the shed this morning," replied Bea. "I think he'd been chased there by Jasper."

King George untangled himself from the mop and bucket, frowning. "Beatrice, please don't tell me you're collecting animals again. I'd hoped you were becoming more sensible— and we're guests here, too. How can you expect Great-Aunt Sylvia to keep tiresome animals in her home?"

Bea went red. "I didn't mean to bring Marshmallow inside, but he was really scared because Jasper was being so fierce. I knew I had to help!"

"It's understandable that she wanted to help the baby reindeer, George," said Uncle Henry.

"Maybe . . . but it's not good manners to bring it inside when we're

guests here," said King George sternly.
"What will it be next? A hotel for
reindeer? A restaurant for beetles? A
holiday home for little mice?"

"Bea found a mouse called Fluff
at home!" Alfie piped up until Bea
nudged him.

Great-Aunt Sylvia walked over,
leaning on her stick, and tickled
Marshmallow under the chin. "There's
no need to worry, George. I'm not
upset about having this reindeer in the
castle in the slightest!"

"That's very kind of you, Aunt, but
Beatrice must put him back outside at
once," said the king. "He can't be allowed
to mess up your beautiful home."

"Nonsense! He's much too small to
be left outside by himself. He needs a
bed of nice warm hay and plenty of

fresh cabbage." Great-Aunt Sylvia leaned closer to Bea, and her brown eyes sparkled. "I'll tell you a secret! When I was your age, I loved looking after animals more than anything else. I once brought a stray kitten into the castle and cared for it until my parents found it another home. It was such an adorable little thing!"

Bea's heart skipped. "Then you really don't mind if Marshmallow stays here tonight?"

"I don't mind at all," said Great-Aunt Sylvia. "But we must keep him apart from Jasper—what a naughty kitty!"

Mr. Upply's shoulders stiffened. "Would you like me to fetch something suitable for the animal to sleep in, Lady Sylvia? I think there's a large wooden crate in the shed that might do."

"Thank you, Upply. We'll turn this castle into an animal hotel in the shake of a reindeer's tail!" Lady Sylvia laughed.

The butler trudged away, sighing deeply. Jasper wriggled a bit in Natasha's arms before closing his eyes and giving one long, deep purr.

Bea gave her great-aunt a hug. "Thank you! I promise I'll look for Marshmallow's herd tomorrow. I hope they're still close by!"

Uncle Henry helped Mr. Upply bring the wooden crate inside, and they set it up in a corner of the library. Bea and Alfie filled the crate with hay that the butler had brought from the shed.

Annie helped by bringing a dish of fresh water and putting it in a corner of the crate. Then she asked Mrs. Miller for some cabbage and spinach in case Marshmallow got hungry. Natasha found a soft blanket for Jasper to sleep on and settled the cat in the kitchen. The door between

the kitchen and the rest of the castle was to be kept firmly closed, just in case Jasper got any ideas about chasing the reindeer again.

Everyone gathered around to see Marshmallow placed in his new home.

Bea gently lowered him onto the hay. The reindeer, who had grown sleepy in Bea's arms, looked very surprised at first. Then he lay down and nibbled a piece of cabbage.

"See his little white tail?" said Alfie. "It's exactly the size of a marshmallow, and that's how I decided what to call him."

"It's not fair that Alfie got to choose his name!" cried Annie.

"You could pick his middle name," suggested Bea. "Lots of people have more than one name. My middle name is Isabel, and Natasha's is Elizabeth."

Annie's face lit up. "Then I'm going to call him Marshmallow Jelly Bean Cocoa Marmaduke Snowball! Do you like it?"

"I think it's brilliant!" Bea smiled

as she put her arm around Annie's shoulder. "Marshmallow Jelly Bean Cocoa Marmaduke Snowball is the cutest little reindeer in the whole kingdom!"

Chapter Nine

Marshmallow
Finds His Family

Bea woke up early the next morning after a long, exciting dream about reindeer. In her dream, the castle had been transformed into an animal sanctuary. There were reindeer everywhere—in the parlor, in the library, and scampering all the way across the palace lawn.

Bea jumped out of bed and peeked through the curtain at the amazing

snowy wonderland outside the castle
window. Icicles hung from the shed
roof, and frost sparkled like diamonds
on the tree branches. Bea smiled as she
spotted the wild, zigzagging footprints
in the snow that she and Natasha had
left the night before. She was so glad
Great-Aunt Sylvia had let Marshmallow
stay in the castle.

Natasha was still sleeping peacefully
with the blanket pulled up to her chin.
Bea put on her furry slippers. Then she
gathered up Leo's birthday presents.
She was determined to fix the torn
wrapping paper and the ribbon right
away. She snipped off the torn pieces of
paper and taped the neat bits together.
Then she trimmed the chewed end from
the teddy bear's ribbon and wrapped
everything up again.

Bea left the neatly wrapped presents on her bed and ran downstairs. Marshmallow bounded to the side of his crate, poking his nose through the gap in the wooden slats.

"Morning, Marshmallow!" Bea stroked his furry brown nose. "Did you sleep well?"

Marshmallow gave a cute little bleating sound and frisked up and down.

Bea smiled. "I'll see if there's some fresh broccoli for you in the kitchen." She hurried down the passage and found Great-Aunt Sylvia filling the kettle at the kitchen sink.

"Hello, Beatrice!" Lady Sylvia smiled. "I'm glad you're up early. Would you like some help finding Marshmallow's herd this morning?"

"Yes, please!" cried Bea. "Do you know where they are?"

"Not exactly, but I saw a reindeer herd close to the woods a few days ago. Why don't you have some breakfast, and then we can take Marshmallow out to find them." Great-Aunt Sylvia picked up a pair of binoculars and

hung them around her neck. "I'm
hoping these will come in handy!"

Bea hurriedly ate a bowl of cereal
before putting on her coat and scarf.
She fetched Marshmallow from his
crate and held him tightly, pressing
her cheek against his pale brown coat.
Suddenly, she didn't want to take
the little reindeer back to his herd. It
had been so wonderful looking after
him, and she would miss him terribly.
But she knew the best place for
Marshmallow was with his family.

Great-Aunt Sylvia was waiting by
the door, dressed in a brightly colored
scarf, a snow coat, and purple boots.
"Let's get going, shall we?" she said briskly.
"If we wait too long, the whole castle will
be awake. And if we take everyone with
us, we'll scare the reindeer herd away."

They set out across the garden, with Bea carrying Marshmallow snuggled up against her coat. The snow crunched under their boots, and the sun shone in the clear blue sky, making everything sparkle.

Great-Aunt Sylvia led Bea through the woods where she'd searched for the reindeer the night before. Robins and blackbirds sang in the trees, and there were little bird tracks in the snow. On the other side of the woods, a cluster of white fields stretched into the distance.

"Here!" Great-Aunt Sylvia handed Bea the binoculars. "Tell me what you see."

Bea held Marshmallow tightly with one arm and put the binoculars to her eyes. At once, everything looked closer and clearer. She turned them slowly sideways, scanning the bright landscape. To the right, there was a cluster of trees and a line of fences edged with snow. To the left, there were some dark brown bushes dotted across a field.

Bea moved the binoculars on. Then

she stopped and swung back to
the bushes. They weren't
bushes at all. They
were reindeer!
"I've found them!
There are lots of
reindeer right
over there."

Lady Sylvia took the binoculars back and checked for herself. "So there are! Then let's get this little one back to his family."

Marshmallow began to bleat, kicking his little legs. Bea held him tight and stroked him until he calmed down. Then she and Great-Aunt Sylvia trekked across the snow toward the reindeer.

As they drew closer, Bea noticed the animals pushing the snow aside and nibbling at the plants underneath. Marshmallow began to bleat again, and several reindeer lifted their heads to look in their direction.

Lady Sylvia lowered her voice to a whisper. "Why don't you move forward from here? Try to get a little closer before you let Marshmallow go. With any luck, his mother will recognize him."

Bea walked on slowly and carefully. More of the reindeer raised their heads to watch her. As soon as she was close, she set Marshmallow down on the snow and gave him one more hug. "Good luck, Marshmallow," she whispered. "I'll never forget you."

The little reindeer nuzzled her cheek before skipping across the field to join the herd. One reindeer with large antlers stepped forward and touched

Marshmallow's back with her nose. Bea smiled in delight. That must be his mother. Marshmallow gave a happy bleat as he snuggled close to her legs, his little tail twitching.

Some of the reindeer started walking and the herd began to move on, with Marshmallow staying close to his mother's side. Bea watched as they all trotted away across the snowy field with their antlers raised high.

When Bea and Great-Aunt Sylvia returned, the castle was full of noise and people rushing to and fro. The dining room was covered with a beautiful red-and-white tablecloth, and a mouth-watering smell was drifting from the kitchen.

"What's happening?" Bea asked

Alfie, as he bounced past with a party hat on his head.

"It's nearly time for Leo's party!" Alfie grinned. "Natasha's been helping Mrs. Miller make the birthday cake. I sneaked in and ate some of the chocolate icing!"

Half an hour later, Mrs. Miller brought out a wonderful chocolate cake with *Happy Birthday, Leo* written in big blue letters. Everyone joined in with singing to the little boy and handing him gifts. Leo chuckled loudly as Aunt Amber helped him open his parcels. He seemed to like the wrapping paper as much as the presents.

Then, as they ate the birthday cake, Uncle Henry asked Bea all about Marshmallow and the reindeer herd.

"We found them just beyond the

woods," said Bea, explaining how they'd spotted the reindeer through the binoculars.

"I wish Marshmallow could have stayed here with us," said Annie sadly.

Aunt Amber hugged Annie. "I know, honey. But he's a wild reindeer, and I'm sure he was very happy to see his family again."

After some party games and a delicious birthday lunch, everyone put on hats, coats, scarves, and gloves and went out into the snowy garden. King George helped Annie make another snowman, along with Natasha, who found some pebbles to make the face.

Bea and Alfie pulled the sled up the hill beyond the garden. Bea stopped at the top, tingling with excitement. She gazed at the fields beyond the wood.

In the distance, tiny brown shapes were moving across the snow.

"Look, Alfie! There's the reindeer herd." She smiled. Marshmallow would be among them—safe and sound with his family again.

"Do you think you'll ever stop finding animals that need help?" Alfie asked her.

"I hope not." Bea laughed. "I love animals, and finding Marshmallow was one of the best adventures of all!"

Paula Harrison is the author of the Rescue Princesses series, the Secret Rescuers series, and the Royal Rescues series. She wanted to be a writer from a young age but spent many happy years being a primary school teacher first. Paula finds inspiration in lots of things, from cloud shapes to snippets of conversation. She loves sandy beaches and eating popcorn. She lives with her husband and children in Buckinghamshire, England, which is nowhere near the sea.

Olivia Chin Mueller grew up in a small town in Connecticut and earned an MFA from the Rhode Island School of Design. She now lives in Rhode Island. When she's not illustrating, Olivia loves playing with her cats, sewing and felting, and collecting cute toys and nail polish.